THE AMERICAN GIRLS

17  74

FELICITY, a spunky, spritely colonial girl,
full of energy and independence

18  24

JOSEFINA, an Hispanic girl whose heart and
hopes are as big as the New Mexico sky

18  54

KIRSTEN, a pioneer girl of strength and
spirit who settles on the frontier

18  64

ADDY, a courageous girl determined to be
free in the midst of the Civil War

19  04

SAMANTHA, a bright Victorian beauty, an
orphan raised by her wealthy grandmother

19  34

KIT, a clever, resourceful girl facing the
Great Depression with spirit and determination

19  44

MOLLY, who schemes and dreams on the
home front during World War Two

1944

CHANGES FOR MOLLY

A Winter Story

BY VALERIE TRIPP

ILLUSTRATIONS NICK BACKES

VIGNETTES KEITH SKEEN

American Girl ™

Published by Pleasant Company Publications
© Copyright 1988, 2000 by Pleasant Company
All rights reserved. No part of this book may be used or reproduced
in any manner whatsoever without written permission except in the
case of brief quotations embodied in critical articles and reviews.
For information, address: Book Editor, Pleasant Company Publications,
8400 Fairway Place, P.O. Box 620998, Middleton, WI 53562.

Printed in the United States of America.
00 01 02 03 04 05 06 07 08 QWT 36 35 34 33 32 31 30 29 28

PICTURE CREDITS
The following individuals and organizations have generously given
permission to reprint images contained in "Looking Back": pp. 62-63—Printed by permission
of the Norman Rockwell Family Trust. © 1945 the Norman Rockwell Family Trust; AP/Wide
World Photos; © Bettmann/CORBIS; Maytag Corporation; H. Armstrong Roberts, Inc.; Ellen
Kaiper Collection, *The Life and Times of Rosie the Riveter*, Miriam Frank, Marilyn Ziebarth, and
Connie Field; pp. 64-65—Harold Carter/LIFE Magazine © 1946 Time Inc.; Joe Scherschel/LIFE
Magazine © Time Inc.; National Archives; photo by Dan Weiner, courtesy Sandra Weiner;
© Bettmann/CORBIS; pp. 66-67—© Bettman/CORBIS; Johnny Florea/LIFE Magazine
© Time Inc.; © CORBIS; National Archives; U.N. Photos.

Edited by Jeanne Thieme
Designed by Myland McRevey and Ingrid Slamer
Art Directed by Kathleen A. Brown
Cover Background by John Pugh

Library of Congress Cataloging-in-Publication Data

Tripp, Valerie, 1951-
Changes for Molly: a winter story
by Valerie Tripp; illustrations, Nick Backes; vignettes, Keith Skeen.

p.cm.—(The American girls collection)
Summary: Molly's excitement at performing in a big show is exceeded
only by the announcement that her father is returning home from the war.
ISBN 0-937295-96-5   ISBN 0-937295-49-3 (pbk.)
I. Backes, Nick, ill. II. Title. III. Series.
PZ7.T7363Ch   1988   [Fic]—dc19   88-19630   CIP   AC

TO KATHERINE HELEN PETTY

TABLE OF CONTENTS

MOLLY'S FAMILY

MOLLY
*A nine-year-old
who is growing up
on the home front
in America during
World War Two.*

DAD
*Molly's father, a doctor
who is somewhere in
England, taking care of
wounded soldiers.*

MOTHER
*Molly's mother, who holds
the family together while
Dad is away.*

JILL
*Molly's fourteen-year-old
sister, who is always
trying to act grown-up.*

RICKY
*Molly's twelve-year-old
brother—a big pest.*

BRAD
*Molly's five-year-old
brother—a little pest.*

MRS. GILFORD
*The housekeeper, who
rules the roost when
Mom is at work.*

LINDA
*One of Molly's best
friends, a practical
schemer.*

SUSAN
*Molly's other best
friend, a cheerful
dreamer.*

HURRAY FOR THE U.S.A.!

Molly McIntire and her friends Linda and Susan stood at the bus stop waiting for the city bus to come and take them home. They had to wait under the movie theater sign because it was a cold, rainy March afternoon. But the girls didn't even notice the rain or the cold. They were too excited. They'd just come from their tap dance lesson at Miss LaVonda's, so they were warm and sweaty.

"Our show is going to be the best show anyone ever saw," said Molly happily.

"I can't wait!" said Susan. "I've never been in a big show like this before."

"Well, there's never *been* a show like this in

Jefferson before," said Linda. "Practically everyone in the whole town has a part in it, singing or dancing or playing in the band."

"Even my mom is in the show," said Molly. "She's going to make a speech about the Red Cross Blood Drive."

"Our part is the best part of all," Susan gloated. "Miss LaVonda said so. She said we're the grand finally."

"The grand finn—*al*—lee," corrected Linda.

"Oh, whatever," said Susan cheerily. "We're the flag. And the flag is the most important thing in the show."

Miss LaVonda, the girls' tap dance teacher, was in charge of a big show called "Hurray for the U.S.A." The show was being put on at the Veterans' Hospital in Jefferson. The hospital was full of soldiers who had been hurt or wounded in the war.

Molly, Linda, Susan, and the rest of the girls in their tap dance class were the very last act in the show. They were going to dance and sing a patriotic song. They would wear red, white, and blue costumes so that together they formed a giant flag on the stage. At one point in the song, the flag would part in the middle and one girl would do a special tap dance all by herself. She was Miss Victory, and her solo dance was a real showstopper.

Miss LaVonda had not picked a girl to be Miss Victory yet. While the girls were rehearsing, she danced that part herself. But during the next week, every girl in the class was going to have a chance to try out to be Miss Victory. Molly already knew the special solo dance by heart.

"I can do that Miss Victory dance in my sleep," she said to Linda and Susan. She closed her eyes, held her umbrella up high, and did the complicated dance steps right there on the sidewalk. Linda and Susan sang the music for her. "Ta da!" she said at the end.

"Gosh!" exclaimed Susan as the girls climbed on the bus. "That was great, Molly. You can make that dance look good even in your galoshes! I'm sure you'll get to be Miss Victory."

"Well," said Molly generously, "everyone gets to try out. Either of you could be Miss Victory, too."

"Nope. Not me," said Linda. She plopped
down in the seat in front of Molly and Susan.
"I'd be too nervous all alone out there in front of
everybody. I'd forget all the hard steps and just
stand there like a dope. I don't want to be Miss
Victory."

"Me either," said Susan. "You'll be Miss Victory,
Molly. Everybody says so."

Molly blushed. She was very pleased. "I sure
would like to be Miss Victory," she said. She tapped
the dance steps on the floor of the bus even though
she was sitting down. "I love the costume."

"Oh, it's gorgeous," agreed Susan.

Miss Victory's costume was made of
shiny blue and red satin and sparkly
silver material. There was a big silver
star on one shoulder, and a star
crown for Miss Victory to wear on
her head.

Linda turned sideways to look back at Molly.
"You *should* be Miss Victory," she said loyally. "You
dance the best, so that would be fair. But sometimes
these things aren't exactly fair."

"What do you mean?" asked Susan. "Miss

LaVonda is fair. And she wants the best dancer to
be Miss Victory, and that's Molly."

"I know, I know," said Linda. She squirmed a
little. "But, well, in a show, a lot depends on how
a person looks, not just how she sings or dances. I
mean, think about that silver star thing Miss Victory
is supposed to wear on her head. It will only look
right on somebody with curly hair. It would look
dumb on somebody with straight hair like mine—"

"Or braids like mine," interrupted Molly
glumly. All her high hopes of being Miss Victory
had fallen with a thud. She knew Linda was right,
as usual.

Linda nodded sadly at Molly. "Yeah, I'm afraid
braids would look dumb, too," she said. "No offense,
Molly."

"Molly has very . . . *normal* hair," said Susan.
"Miss LaVonda won't care."

"No, Linda is right," said Molly. "Miss Victory
should have beautiful curls. My hair is just brown
sticks." She pulled her slicker hat down over her ears
and looked out the window at the weepy rain.

"Well, there's no point in getting upset about it,"
said Linda kindly. "Let's face it. Your hair is just

plain straight. It comes out of your head that way. You can't do anything about it."

"Oh yes you can," said Susan. "My sister Gloria's hair is really sort of clumpy, but she gave herself a home permanent wave, and now she has lots of curls."

Molly was interested. "Gloria gave herself a permanent?" she asked.

"Yeah, sure! It was easy," said Susan breezily. "You just get a box of permanent lotion and you wash your hair—or maybe you don't wash your hair, I forget. Anyway, you put the lotion on and set your hair on these special sort of curlers, and then it dries and you take the curlers out and you have all these beautiful curls."

Linda looked doubtful. "I don't know," she said. "My aunt gave herself one of those home permanents, and she ended up looking like a French poodle."

"It doesn't matter anyway," said Molly. "My mother would never let me have a permanent wave."

"Well, she wouldn't need to know until afterwards," Susan pointed out. "And by that time you'd already have the curls."

Molly thought about that as the girls climbed off the bus at their stop. "Does the home permanent kit cost a lot?" she asked.

"I don't think so," said Susan. "You could use your Saturday movie money."

"That wouldn't be enough," said Linda.

"Well, then I'll chip in *my* movie money," Susan said firmly. "Molly needs to get curls."

Linda looked at Molly. "Do you really want a permanent?"

"I really want to be Miss Victory," Molly answered slowly. "And it does seem like a permanent might help. So . . ."

"Okay," said Linda. "I'll chip in my movie money, too. But I'm still not sure about this permanent wave business. It seems risky to me."

"Oh, don't worry, Linda," said Susan. "I know all about it. I'll give Molly the permanent. It will look gorgeous. You'll see."

When Molly got home, Brad was sitting at the kitchen table coloring and Mom was helping Ricky with his homework.

"Hello, dear," said Mrs. McIntire. "Leave your

galoshes on the newspaper by the door, please. Mrs. Gilford just washed the floor today. How was tap dancing?"

"Fine," said Molly. She was thinking so hard about getting a permanent that she was frowning.

Mrs. McIntire looked up. "Why so glum, chum? You're usually so happy after dancing class."

"She must have caught sight of herself in a mirror," said Ricky. "Yikes! That would make *anyone* glum."

"Har dee har har," said Molly. "That's so funny I forgot to laugh."

"Well, I have something that will cheer us all up," said Mom. "It's a letter from Dad. I've been waiting for everyone to be home before I read it. Ricky, call Jill. Let's all go into the living room."

When everyone was settled, Mom began. "Dear Merry McIntires . . ." Suddenly, she stopped. "Oh!" she exclaimed.

"What? What is it?" everyone asked.

Mrs. McIntire's face was glowing. She tried hard to keep her voice calm, but it was so full of happiness it sounded wobbly. She read, "I'm coming home . . ." and everyone exploded.

"HURRAY! YIPPEEE! DAD! DAD! DAD!"

Molly danced around the room with Jill. Ricky cheered, "Yahoo! Hurray!" Brad hugged his mother, who was wiping tears from her eyes.

"Settle down now!" said Mrs. McIntire, laughing. "Don't you want to hear the rest?"

Everyone got quiet and listened as she read:

```
My orders  have been changed.  I'm
coming back to the States to take care
of the wounded soldiers there.  I'll work
at the Veterans' Hospital in Jefferson,
so I'll be able to live  at home. Of
course, no one can tell me for sure
exactly when I'll get home. But right
now, it looks like I might be there by
the eighteenth of March. Maybe in time
for lunch!

     It will be so wonderful to see all
of you!  I can tell by the pictures you
sent that Ricky is probably a basketball
star by now, and Brad isn't a baby any-
more. And Jill! You look so grown-up and
sophisticated in your prom dress!  You've
become a beauty just like your mother.
And of course, I can't wait to see good
old olly Molly and taste Mrs. Gilford's
perfect pot roast. I'll be so glad to
get home!  Hurray for the U.S.A.!

          Lots of love,
```

Dad

9

Mrs. McIntire read, "I'm coming home . . ."
and everyone exploded.

"Well!" exclaimed Mrs. McIntire as everyone cheered again. "Well! I can hardly believe it! This is the news we've been waiting for ever since Dad left!"

"And March eighteenth is only two weeks from now," said Jill.

"Oh, it will be so great to have him home again!" said Molly.

"How will Dad get here?" asked Brad.

"I'm not sure," said Mrs. McIntire. "I guess he'll come on the train."

"I think we'd better pick him up at the station," said Brad. "He might not remember where our house is."

"Don't worry, dear," said Mrs. McIntire. "I'm sure Dad will find us."

"Let's phone Gram and Granpa and tell them the good news!" said Jill.

"Good idea!" said Mrs. McIntire. She started to put the letter back in the envelope.

"Oh, may I see the letter?" asked Molly. She wanted to read it by herself. It was such wonderful news! Dad was coming home!

She read along and came to the last paragraph,

where Dad said Ricky was a basketball star, Brad had grown up, Jill was a sophisticated beauty, and Molly . . . Molly was just good old olly Molly, mentioned in the same sentence as pot roast.

Molly felt disappointed and a little hurt. Dad sounded so pleased and proud of the way everyone else had changed. But he didn't say anything about how *she* had changed at all. Did he think she was just the same dumb little kid she'd been when he left? She would have to show him that she had grown up, that she was different now, so that he would be proud of *her*, too. But how could she do it?

Molly began to have a wonderful idea. The show! The "Hurray for the U.S.A." show! Dad would be home in time to see it. What if Dad saw her on the stage, in front of a huge audience, dancing the special Miss Victory solo dance, looking beautiful in the sparkly costume, wearing the silver crown on top of long, lovely curls? *Then* he would see she was grown-up and different! He'd be so surprised and proud!

Right then Molly made up her mind. She would get a permanent wave so that she would have curls. She would be Miss Victory. And Dad would see her in the show, looking beautiful.

Everything would be perfect.

A HAIR-RAISING EXPERIENCE

That night, Molly couldn't sleep. *Dad's coming home, Dad's coming home,* she kept thinking. She felt the excitement growing, growing, growing inside until she thought she'd burst with happiness.

She kept imagining how it would be when Dad saw her in the show. She would be wearing the glamorous Miss Victory costume. All the lights would be shining on her. Silver stars would sparkle in her curly hair. Dad would watch her do the complicated tap dance. Afterwards, backstage, Dad would say, "Why, Molly! You've changed so much. You're so grown-up and sophisticated! Just as much as Jill!" Then they'd all come home and celebrate.

Molly went through the wonderful imaginary scene again and again.

Molly rolled over and stared up at the ceiling. What would it be like to have Dad home again after he'd been away at war for two years? What would it be like to have him back in the house? Molly could remember the warm, vanilla-y smell of his pipe tobacco and the sound of his voice calling out, "I'm home!" at the end of the day. But Dad's face was a little blurry in her memory. She scrunched up her eyes and tried to picture Dad's face clearly— the way he really looked, not the way he looked in his Army uniform in the shadowy black-and-white snapshots he sent from England. She couldn't seem to see him.

Finally, Molly got out of bed and tiptoed down-stairs to the living room to look at the old photo albums. She sat cross-legged on the couch, holding the biggest album on her lap. She stared and stared at the pictures pasted to the black pages. There was a funny one of Dad painting the garage. He looked so tall and handsome and happy. On the next page, there was a picture of the whole family together, taken at Thanksgiving a few months before Dad left for the war. It was very discouraging. *Everyone but me looks so different now,* thought Molly. *I look exactly the same now as I did then. Just plain old me.*

"Molly!" she heard Mom say. "I *thought* I saw a light down here. Why are you up?"

"I couldn't sleep," said Molly. "I keep thinking about Dad coming home."

"Me, too," said Mom. She sat next to Molly on the couch.

"It's so wonderful that he'll be home on the eighteenth of March," said Molly. "He can see all of us in the show."

"Now, Molly," said Mom. "Don't go getting your hopes up. Dad said he *might* be here on the eighteenth. But the Army often changes plans at the last minute. I'm sure Dad will do his best to get here in time for the show, but you can't count on it."

Molly knew Mom was being sensible, but she was still sure Dad would be home in time to see her as Miss Victory. It would just be so perfect! She didn't want to hear any discouraging warnings, so she said, "I sort of couldn't remember what Dad

looked like. That's why I got out the old albums."

Mom held half the album on her lap. She looked at the Thanksgiving picture. "Granpa took this picture. I remember that day very well," she said. "There I am in my polka dot dress. It was new back then. I still wear that dress sometimes. It doesn't look so stylish anymore." She sighed, "Neither do I, I'm afraid." She pushed a lock of hair behind one ear. "Look at Brad! He was just a baby. He looks so different now."

"Do you think Dad will look different?" asked Molly.

"Mmmm, yes, he probably will," said Mom. "He'll probably look a little thinner and a little older, just as I do."

"Do you think he'll act different?" Molly asked.

"I don't know," said Mom. "He has seen some very sad and terrible things during the war. War does change people. It doesn't just happen and then disappear, all forgiven and forgotten. War leaves scars on people, and not just the kind of scars you can see. But I think Dad will still be our same old Dad at heart. He'll still love us. We'll all have to get used to one another again. It may take some time. We're all older. We're all different."

"I sure want Dad to see that I'm different," said Molly. "I want him to see that I'm grown-up now, not just a plain dumb kid anymore. But the problem is, I don't *look* different."

Mom hugged Molly. "Your dad will be so happy to see you, he won't care what you look like," she said. "You know he'll always love you and be proud of you, no matter what."

"Mothers always say that," said Molly.

"Because it's true!" said Mrs. McIntire with a smile. "And here's another thing mothers always say: Get to bed! Tomorrow is a school day. Besides, it's cold down here. You don't want to greet Dad with a red nose and sniffles, do you? Come on, now. Off to bed. Lickety-split!"

"Okay," said Molly. She hugged her mother and went back upstairs, carrying the photo album with her. *I WILL look different though,* she said to herself. *I can't wait to get that permanent.*

However, Molly did have to wait. She had to wait two more days, until Saturday, when she and Linda and Susan got their movie money. The movie cost twenty-five cents, and they all got nickels for popcorn. Susan's mother always gave her an extra nickel in case of emergency. Luckily, Molly had thirty cents left over from a dollar Granpa had given her for Christmas, so they had just enough money. The permanent wave kit cost $1.25.

"It's really nice of you to give up your movie money," Molly said to Linda and Susan as the girls headed to the drugstore.

"Well," said Linda, "I hear this movie has lots of kissing and mushy stuff in it, so I don't care about missing it." Linda liked cowboy and Indian movies.

"*Besides*," said Susan, "your dad is coming home. This is going to be the most important moment of your whole and entire life so far! You've got to have those curls. Not just to be Miss Victory, but to show your dad how grown-up and sophisticated you are. It's so exciting!"

Molly nodded. "I can't believe he's finally coming home, after all this time," she said.

"You're so lucky, Molly," said Susan. "Your father's coming home safe and sound."

"Yeah, not like Grace Littlefield's father," said Linda. Mr. Littlefield's legs had been wounded in the war, and he would never walk again.

"Poor Grace," said Molly softly.

"It would be terrible to have a father who couldn't walk anymore," said Susan.

"I bet Grace is just happy he's home and alive," said Linda. "Think about Miss Campbell."

All the girls got quiet. Their third grade teacher, Miss Campbell, had been engaged to marry a soldier who was killed during the summer.

"I wonder if Miss Campbell's soldier ever thought he might be killed and be dead forever and never get to marry Miss Campbell," said Susan.

"Every soldier knows he might get killed," said Molly. "That's why every soldier is a hero."

"Yeah, but it seems to me that once they're killed, they just go to heaven where everything is fine," said Linda. "It's the people left behind on earth who love them that have a harder time. They're sad, but they have to go on with the rest of their lives. I think Miss Campbell is as much a hero as her soldier was."

"But she can be proud of the sacrifice she made for her country," said Susan.

"I think I would be more sad than proud if my dad got killed," said Molly.

"Me, too," said Susan.

"Me, too," said Linda. "I'd sure rather be happy and have the person I love home safe and sound than be proud because he died a hero."

"Yeah," said Molly. "Well, at least the war is supposed to be almost over. Our soldiers have pushed all the way into Germany. Mom says the Nazis have to surrender soon."

"I sort of don't get it," said Susan. "How do they decide when a war is over? Does one side change its mind and say it was wrong and then surrender?"

"No," said Linda. "A war is over when one side gives up because so many of its soldiers are killed it can't fight anymore."

"Oh," said Susan. "Well, it'll be great to have all the fighting end. I can hardly remember what it was like before the war. When it ends, everything will be wonderful."

"It seems like everything should be wonderful," said Linda. "But I don't see how it can be when so many people will be sad about their dads and friends and everyone who got killed or wounded."

"That's why our 'Hurray for the U.S.A.' show is so important," said Molly. "It's a way to show the wounded men that we're glad they are alive and to thank them for being so brave."

"That's right!" said Susan.

"It doesn't seem like very much, but I guess it's the best we can do," agreed Linda.

By now they were standing outside the door of the drugstore. "Now, when we go in, you'd better let me do all the talking," said Susan, "because I know about the permanent."

"Okay," said Molly and Linda. They gave all their money to Susan, and she led them inside.

The shelves seemed fuller these days, now that there was less rationing. In the hair care section, there were lots of different shampoos and more than one kind of home permanent kit. Susan read one of the boxes. It said, "Big, Beautiful, Bouncy Curls for the New You."

"Oh, this is definitely the one we want," Susan said. "So you can be the New You. The New Molly."

"Better get the extra-strong formula," said Linda, "because Molly has long hair."

As Susan was paying for the kit, the drugstore man said, "Does your mother know you're using this?"

"Oh, it's not for *me*," said Susan innocently. "It's for someone . . . older." That was true. Molly's birthday was two months before Susan's.

The three girls rushed out of the store and hurried back to Molly's house. They had decided to give Molly the permanent wave in their secret hide-out, the room above the garage.

Susan dragged a rickety old chair into the

"Oh, this is definitely the one we want," Susan said.
"So you can be the New You. The New Molly."

middle of the room. "Here," she said to Molly. "Sit on this. It'll be just like a beauty parlor." She wrapped a dusty sheet around Molly's shoulders.

"Some beauty parlor! For one thing, it's freezing cold up here," shivered Linda. "And how are you going to shampoo her hair? We don't have any water."

"Oh, we can skip that part," said Susan. She began to unbraid Molly's hair.

"No we can't skip it," said Linda. "It says right here on the box: 'First, shampoo hair.'"

"That's probably only if your hair is dirty," said Susan. "Molly's hair is pretty clean already. Gosh, it sure is straight, Molly! And it's kind of long. Maybe we should cut it a little bit, so the curlers can hold it better."

Molly felt nervous. She began to suspect Susan didn't really know what she was doing. "I think we'd better not cut my hair," she said. "If we did, Mom would be really mad."

"Okay," said Susan. "I don't have any scissors anyway. Now let's see. I guess it's time to put the waving lotion on your hair." She opened the bottle of lotion. A terrible smell filled the room.

"P.U.!" exclaimed Linda. "That stuff smells awful!"

"It smells like a wet dog!" said Molly. "I don't want to smell like *that!*"

"Oh, for heaven's sake!" said Susan. "If you want curls, you're just going to have to put up with the smell. I'm sure it wears off after a while."

"Maybe this bottle of lotion has gone bad or something," said Linda. She was pinching her nose between two fingers. "Did the waving lotion Gloria used smell like this?"

"I don't know," said Susan.

"You don't know? Weren't you there when she gave herself the permanent?" asked Molly.

"Not *exactly*," said Susan. "I mean, I didn't exactly watch her do the whole thing. I saw her with the curlers in her hair, and I saw her after, when she took the curlers out."

"Susan!" groaned Molly. "You don't know how to do this at all, do you?"

"Of course I do," snapped Susan. "Anybody can read the directions on the box and kind of figure it out as you go along."

"Oh, brother!" said Linda. "Molly's probably going to end up bald!"

"She will not—" Susan began.

Just then, the door swung open and Jill burst in. "What are you guys doing up here?" she asked.

"Uh, just playing," said Molly. "What are you doing up here?"

"I came to . . ." said Jill. She stopped talking and sniffed the air. "Gosh! It reeks in here! What are you . . . ?" She looked at Molly sitting in the chair with her hair down. Then she frowned and squinted at Molly. "Molly McIntire, it smells like permanent wave lotion in here. You're not letting Linda and

27

Susan give you a permanent, are you?"

Molly, Linda, and Susan were silent.

"Don't do it, Molly," said Jill. "Really, it's not that easy to do it right, and it'll look horrible if it comes out wrong. You'll regret it, you really will."

"But I *need* curly hair," wailed Molly. "I have to have it for the show, and for Dad, and everything. I just absolutely have to."

Jill sighed. "A permanent isn't the way to get curls. With hair like yours, it will just give you wrinkles and frizz. Listen, I can understand why you want to look good. I'll even help you. I'll set your hair every night between now and the show if that's what you want. I promise."

"Really?" asked Molly.

"Really," said Jill.

Molly was relieved. "Gee," she said. "Thanks, Jill. That will be much better."

"Yeah," said Linda. "We sort of knew we were getting in over our heads with this permanent business. Get it?"

Even Susan had to laugh. Molly was very glad the hair-raising experience was over.

CHAPTER THREE

—

THE NEW MOLLY

Sunday night, Jill and Molly began work on the New Molly. Molly didn't even have to remind Jill of her promise. After dinner, Jill said, "Come on, Molly. Let's go up to my room."

"What are you two drips up to?" asked Ricky.

"None of your beeswax," answered Molly as she followed Jill upstairs.

Molly sat perfectly still on the stool at Jill's vanity table. Jill draped a towel around her shoulders and undid her braids, brushing out the tangles with long, smooth strokes. She took a few strands and wrapped them around her hand, trying to make them curve under. They just flopped.

Molly sighed. "See?" she said. "It's hopeless."

"No it's not," said Jill. "We'll set it in pin curls. It'll be fine."

Slowly and patiently, Jill twisted strands of hair into curlicues and pinned the curlicues with criss-crossed bobby pins. The curlicues were so tight, Molly's scalp felt as if someone were pulling her hair. The bald spots in between pin curls felt bare and cold. But Molly didn't dare make a peep of complaint. First of all, Jill might get mad and stop. Second of all, maybe it *had* to hurt for it to work.

Jill was quite expert. She held the twisted hair

with one hand and opened the bobby pins by pulling them apart with her front teeth. Molly watched her in the mirror. Dad was right. Jill *was* very pretty and sophisticated-looking.

"Jill, how did you learn how to do all this stuff?" asked Molly.

"Oh, my friend Dolores taught me how to set hair ages ago," said Jill. "Tilt your head a little bit forward, so I can reach the hair near your neck."

"I don't mean just how to set hair," said Molly. "I mean, how come your shirt always stays tucked in? And how come your elbows aren't scabby? And your socks wrinkle just right? How did you learn to look so sophisticated, like Dad said in his letter?" Molly was kind of afraid Jill might laugh, but she didn't.

"I don't know," said Jill. "I guess it comes naturally when you get older."

Molly sighed. "Even if I wore your exact same clothes, I still wouldn't look grown-up."

"You can't make it happen faster than it's going to happen," said Jill. "And you shouldn't try, anyway." She met Molly's eyes in the mirror. "Sometimes I'm sorry because I think the war made all of us grow up too fast. We had to kind of hurry into being serious. And I feel cheated, because Dad missed seeing us through some of the parts of being kids. He wasn't here to teach Brad how to ride a two-wheeler or to help me with algebra. I think you're lucky. At least you have a few more years of being a kid with him."

"I never thought of it that way," said Molly. "I want Dad to think I've changed, that I'm *not* just a dumb kid anymore."

Jill thought a moment. "Even if you don't look different, you *have* changed," she said.

"Really?" asked Molly. "I have? Like how, for instance?"

"Well," said Jill, "the most obvious thing is that you *want* to be different. Gosh, you used to always want everything to be the same as before the war, which was really childish because things can't ever stay the same, especially when there's a war. Remember the fight we had about decorating the Christmas tree? You just wouldn't admit Christmas was going to have to be different with Dad away. This year you were more willing to change."

Jill opened up another bobby pin with her teeth

and then went on thoughtfully, "And you don't clomp around the house the way you used to all the time. You're quieter. And I thought you grew up a lot and learned to think about other people when that English girl, Emily, came to stay with us. You were very generous with her. You definitely act more grown-up now than you did before."

"But I want to *look* grown-up," said Molly.

"Okay," Jill laughed. "That's what we're working on here! But I still think Dad will mostly care that you act older. You really do act more mature."

"Mature!" Molly was terribly flattered. "Mature" was one of Jill's highest words of praise. The opposite—"immature"—was her harshest criticism. Molly sat up very straight. It made her proud that Jill thought she was mature.

"You're done," said Jill. "Try not to wiggle around too much when you sleep or the bobby pins will fall out."

"Okay," said Molly. "Thanks a lot, Jill." She walked slowly down the hall to her bedroom, holding her neck stiff, as if she were balancing a bowl of water on her head.

Suddenly, Ricky jumped in front of her. "Help! Save us!" he shrieked. "It's a porcupine monster from outer space!" He clutched his head and pretended to faint from fear at the sight of her.

Molly was about to sock him. Then she thought of what Jill had said and stopped herself. She just kept walking and sighed, "How immature," leaving Ricky slumped against the wall behind her.

Sleeping on pin curls was like sleeping on thorns. Molly tried putting her face in the pillow, but then she couldn't breathe. She tried wadding up her pillow under her neck instead of under her head, but that made her neck hurt. The pins seemed to find a way to dig into her scalp no matter what she did.

The next morning Molly's head was groggy from no sleep. Her scalp was sore. Her neck was stiff. She had funny red wrinkles on her face and marks from the bobby pins pressed into her cheeks. But it was all worth it, because when Jill took the bobby pins out, Molly's hair was—NOT STRAIGHT.

"Oh, Jill!" exclaimed Molly. "It's wonderful!"

Jill pursed her lips and studied Molly's hair with a critical eye. "We'll try it a different way tonight," she said. "This is okay, but it's more ripply than curly."

But Molly was very pleased with her new look. And at school, all the girls oohed and ahhed when she pushed back the hood on her jacket. She hadn't worn her hat. She was afraid it would crush her hair. So her ears were pink with both cold *and* pleasure when Susan said, "Gosh, Molly! You look like a movie star!"

Linda didn't go that far, but even she had a compliment. "If you took off your glasses, you'd look at least twelve years old, maybe even thirteen," she said seriously.

All day long, Molly was careful not to move her head too much. Every few moments, she'd reach back to touch the ripples with her fingers, to be sure they were still there. Her hair stayed ripply right up to the time for tap dance class. When Miss LaVonda saw her, she smiled. "Why, Molly! Don't you look darling!" Molly's heart lifted.

This was the week everyone got to try out to be

Miss Victory. That day, Alison Hargate did the
special dance first. Linda and Molly watched as
Alison walked up the bleacher steps to take her
position before the music started. The Miss Victory
costume fit her perfectly. Alison's hair was so blond
and her eyes were so blue, she seemed to glow
and light up the stage even without the spotlights
shining on her.

"Gee, she looks great, doesn't she?" whispered
Molly.

Linda shrugged.

When the music started, the girls who were
stars and stripes sang and danced their parts without a mistake. But Alison started the solo too late
and had to hurry down the bleacher steps, so she
was out of step with the music. Her feet seemed to
get all tangled up. As she danced on she did better,
but she seemed very glad when the music was
finally over.

Linda poked Molly and rolled her eyes. "She
may look good, but she sure can't dance as well as
you can," she said.

Miss LaVonda made them all do the whole
dance over and over while other girls tried out for

the solo. Molly danced better every time. Having
the ripples bounce up and down on her back felt
wonderful. There was only one problem. As she
danced, she got more sweaty, and the ripples began
to unravel and droop in a discouraged way. By the
end of class, the beautiful ripples had pretty much
disappeared, and Molly was left with a scraggly
mess of straight, sticky hair.

Unfortunately, the same thing happened every
day. It didn't matter what Jill did to curl Molly's
hair. She tried twisting it around rags,
rolling it up in a hair net, gooing it up
with cream, and drenching it with hair
lacquer. When Molly woke up in
the morning, she would have waves,
ripples, and even curls. But as soon as she danced,
her hair would straighten itself out and hang as limp
as wet noodles. In the war against her hair, Molly
was losing. And she was sure she'd never get to be
Miss Victory unless she and Jill could find a way to
make the curls stay curly.

Finally, it was Friday night, the night before
Molly's turn to try out to be Miss Victory. She and
Jill were desperate. "Okay," said Jill, as if she were

a general preparing for an all-out attack on the enemy. "There's one last thing to try—the wet hair method." Jill wet Molly's hair, twisted it up into tight pin curls, then wet it again. Molly had to sleep with a towel over her pillow, her hair was so wet. The next morning, Molly went off to tap dance class with her damp hair still in the pin curls. "Don't take the bobby pins out until the very last minute," warned Jill.

It was a bitterly cold day. Molly was afraid the pin curls would freeze solid as she hurried along the sidewalk. Her whole head felt like an ice cube. But when she got to class and carefully took out all the pins, her hair had dried and she had glorious, wavy curls. Susan helped her fasten the Miss Victory star on her head.

"Oh, Molly!" Susan gasped. "You look absolutely perfect!"

Molly looked in the mirror. She couldn't help smiling. She did look perfect, except for one thing— her glasses. She took them off and put them inside one of her regular shoes. She knew the dance so well, she wouldn't need those glasses.

38

Anyway, they belonged to the old Molly, not this new, sophisticated Molly dressed in the gorgeous, sparkly Miss Victory costume.

Molly took her place at the top of the bleacher steps as the music began. Everything was a little fuzzy in front of her, but that just made it easier to imagine there was a big crowd watching her. Molly pretended that in the very front row, smiling and clapping, was the most important person of all: Dad.

At exactly the right moment, Molly danced down the steps in perfect time with the music. She danced better than she ever had before. It was as if the music was in her feet, making them light, moving them along through all the fancy steps without a bit of effort from Molly. After the dance, all the girls clapped and cheered for Molly. Linda and Susan clapped the loudest.

"Well!" said Miss LaVonda. "It seems we all agree that Molly should be Miss Victory. Congratulations, Molly! You did a fine job!"

She handed Molly a small plaid suitcase with a silver buckle. "You may use this suitcase to carry the Miss Victory costume back and forth from

"Well!" said Miss LaVonda.
"It seems we all agree that Molly should be Miss Victory."

home to class. Take good care of that costume. You've certainly earned the privilege of wearing it!"

All the girls clapped again, and Molly heard Susan cheer, "Hurray for Molly! Molly is Miss Victory!" Molly thought it was probably the most perfect moment she'd ever had in her life—so far.

CHAPTER
FOUR

THE SHOW
MUST GO ON

Just one more week until Dad comes home! Just one more week until the show! That was all Molly could think about. She was so happy, she danced everywhere, all the time. She danced along the sidewalk on the way to school. She danced in the lunch line. She danced off to rehearsals. She danced sitting down at the dinner table. Her feet were so full of excitement, she just couldn't keep them still.

"Olly Molly, you have turned into a jumping bean," her mother said early in the week. "You never stop moving."

"I can't help it, Mom," said Molly.

Mom shook her head and smiled. "I know

how you feel. Whenever I think about Dad coming home, I feel all fluttery with excitement, too. I just don't show it as much. Your face is all pink with it!" She brushed Molly's bangs from her forehead, then she frowned. "You're a bit feverish, dear. Do you feel all right?"

"Sure!" said Molly. Her throat was a little sore, but she figured that was from singing so much during rehearsals for the show.

Mom stared at Molly. "Your eyes look funny, too—as if you're coming down with something. I don't want you to go to bed with wet hair any-more this week. Is that understood? You'll catch a terrible cold."

"But, Mom—" Molly began.

"But, Molly," Mom said. "You don't want to be sick, do you?"

"No, but—"

"No buts about it. No more wet hair until right before the show. That's that," said Mom firmly.

When Mom sounded like that, there was no point in arguing. So Molly had to go back to her boring old braids for the rest of the week. Actually, it was kind of a relief. Molly's nose was sort of runny. She was afraid she *might* be catching a cold. Besides, her scalp needed a rest from being a prickly cactus.

But Saturday, the day before the show, there was going to be a dress rehearsal. Miss LaVonda said they would practice the whole show in their costumes, just like the real thing. So Mom let Molly sleep with wet hair Friday night and keep her pin curls damp on Saturday morning. "Wear a hat," Mom warned as they all got ready to go to the rehearsal. "Or you'll have icicles dangling down your back instead of curls!"

Molly, Linda, and Susan felt lucky that their act was last because that meant they'd be able to watch almost the whole show while they waited to go on stage. There was a lot of confusion before the dress rehearsal finally began. The three girls sat in their seats watching Miss LaVonda herd all the nervous participants into their places.

The show began with Alison's mother, Mrs. Hargate, singing "The Star-Spangled Banner." She wore a fancy dress made out of shimmery green material. It draped around her, leaving one shoulder bare.

"Gee whiz, she looks like the Statue of Liberty in that dress," whispered Linda. "Do you think she chose it on purpose?"

Mrs. Hargate stretched out the high notes so much, the windows seemed to shake. It made Molly's throat hurt just to listen. "Poor Alison," murmured Susan. "I'd die of embarrassment if *my* mother sang like that in front of all my friends."

Everyone in the auditorium, especially Alison, relaxed with a sigh when Mrs. Hargate finally sang, "And the hooooooome of the braaaaaaave!" But Mrs. Hargate looked very pleased as she walked slowly off the stage.

The next act was more lively. It was the Jefferson Junior High School Band. "Look! There's Ricky with the rest of the tubas!" Molly said to Linda and Susan. Ricky and the other tuba players turned their tubas from side to side as they played so that the huge, shiny horns flashed gold under the spotlights. After the band, some little kids gave a skit about buying War Bonds. Brad was in the skit. He held up a big sign that said "BUY."

Next, the mayor of Jefferson spoke. At the end
of his speech, he introduced Mrs. McIntire, who
asked people to donate blood to the Red Cross
Blood Drive. Molly held her handkerchief up to her
nose the whole time her mother was speaking. She
was afraid she might sneeze and make her mother
forget what she was supposed to say. But she
needn't have worried. Mrs. McIntire seemed very
calm up on the stage. She gave her message in a
loud, clear voice, then she sat down.

"Your mom was great!" said Linda.

"Sure," said Molly as she blew her nose. She
was very proud of her mother. Dad would be proud
and surprised, too. Before the war, Mom would have
been much too shy to make a speech. Now she
thought nothing of it.

The church choir sang hymns next. Jill was in
the choir, but Molly couldn't stay to listen. She and
Linda and Susan had to go backstage to put on
their costumes. Molly was very glad to take the
bobby pins out of her hair because her head ached
so badly. But as she pinned the shiny
crown to her glorious curls, she
forgot all about her headache. She

shivered with excitement and anticipation.

"Here goes!" whispered Linda as she and the other stars and stripes took their places.

The audience gasped, "Oh!" when the curtain went up and the giant flag of dancing girls filled the stage. And when Molly danced down the bleacher steps in her sparkly Miss Victory costume, the audience burst into loud, excited applause. They whooped and cheered and sang along with the music.

Molly couldn't actually see the audience without her glasses, but she could hear them and feel their happy enthusiasm. She danced and twirled and tapped and spun, doing every step perfectly, in a sort of haze of happiness. When she was through, everyone in the audience stood up and cheered for a long time. They kept on cheering even after the curtain was lowered, so the stage hands had to raise the curtain again.

When the curtain finally came down and stayed down, Miss LaVonda rushed out onto the stage and hugged Molly. "You looked perfect and you danced perfectly!" she said. "The audience loved you! And this wasn't even the real audience. If you do as well

*Molly danced and twirled and tapped and spun,
doing every step perfectly, in a sort of haze of happiness.*

tomorrow night, you'll bring down the house!"

Molly beamed. She wasn't sure what Miss LaVonda meant about "bringing down the house," but she figured it was a very good thing for an act to do. She couldn't wait until the next night. Miss LaVonda would see: Molly would dance even *better* when Dad was in the audience!

It was late when the McIntires got home from the rehearsal. Molly was very, very tired all over. Her head felt heavy. It was hard to hold it up while Jill set her hair in wet pin curls before they went to bed. Molly felt weak and shivery. *I am NOT sick,* she said to herself. *I'm just tired. I'll be fine tomorrow because tomorrow is the day Dad's coming home. TOMORROW!*

But Molly's head still felt heavy the next morning when she woke up. Her throat was sore. Her nose was completely stuffed up. Every time she swallowed, her ears really hurt. Every muscle ached. *I'll feel better after breakfast,* Molly thought as she dragged herself out of bed.

But she could only pick at her breakfast. It hurt too much to swallow. She was sipping her orange juice very, very slowly when Brad burst into the kitchen. He was dressed in his best suit. "Can you tie my tie for me, Mom?" he asked.

"Why, Brad!" exclaimed Mrs. McIntire as she turned from the sink. "Don't you look handsome! But isn't it a little early to be dressed up for the show?"

"I'm dressed up for Dad," said Brad.

"Well, I don't think Dad will be here until late this afternoon, if he gets here at all today," said Mrs. McIntire. "We still haven't heard from him yet."

"I want to be ready no matter what," said Brad.

Molly and Mrs. McIntire laughed. "All right," said Mom. "But remember, this is your only good suit. Put your napkin in your collar so you don't spill on it. You'll have to stay tidy all day."

Then Mrs. McIntire turned to Molly and said, "I know you're excited, too, about Dad *and* the show, Molly. But you've got to eat your breakfast. You can't dance on an empty stomach."

"I'm just not hungry," said Molly.

"Not hungry?" said Mom. She immediately put her hand on Molly's forehead. "Molly! You're burning up with fever! Oh, I never should have allowed this wet hair nonsense! Come back upstairs with me. I'm going to take your temperature."

"I'm *not* sick, Mom," protested Molly. Her voice sounded hoarse. "I'm sure I don't have a temperature."

"We'll see," said Mom as she led Molly upstairs.

It turned out that Molly did have a temperature, a high one. "Oh, no," murmured Mrs. McIntire as she looked at the thermometer. "One hundred and three degrees. You'd better get back into your pajamas, dear. Why don't you get into my bed to rest? I'm going to call the doctor."

By now Molly felt so sick she was almost glad to get into Mom's bed and rest her cheek on the cool pillow. *It's probably a good idea to sleep a lot this morning,* she thought. *That way I'll be in good shape for the show this afternoon.*

When the doctor came, he asked Molly to say "ahh" as he looked down her throat. Then he looked into her ears and frowned. "Hmph!" he said. "You've got a very bad ear infection, young lady. You'll have to take this medicine three times a

51

day. And get plenty of sleep. I'll come to see you tomorrow."

Mrs. McIntire followed the doctor into the hallway. Molly could hear them talking softly together outside the door. Then Mrs. McIntire came back in and sat on the bed.

"Well, Molly," Mom said sadly, "the doctor says you *must* stay in bed until the fever goes away. He says you can't go anywhere today."

Molly sat up. "Mom," she said, "I'll stay in bed as much as you want after the show. I promise. But I have to get up this afternoon. I can't be sick in bed when Dad comes home. And I've absolutely *got* to be in the show. I'm Miss Victory."

Mom sighed. "I'm sorry, dear. I can't allow you to be in the show. You're just too sick. I'll have to call Miss LaVonda and tell her she has to find someone else to take your part."

Molly felt too terrible to protest anymore. She rolled over and buried her face in the pillow. Mom rubbed her back. "I know how disappointed you are," she said. "I'm very sorry it had to happen this way, today of all days. I can't think of anything that would be more sad for you, and I can't think of

52

anything to say to make it better." She was quiet for a while, then she said, "Try to get some rest," and left to call Miss LaVonda.

Molly hunched herself into a ball. All of her ached with sickness and sadness and awful disappointment. All of her hopes, all of her wonderful plans, *everything* was ruined! Finally, she couldn't help it. She began to cry. She cried until she fell asleep.

A long time later, in the afternoon, she woke up when someone opened the door to the bedroom. It was Ricky.

"Hi," he said glumly. "Guess what? We just got this telegram from Dad. Here, look." He tossed the yellow telegram to Molly. It said:

```
Travel plans changed. Don't know
when I'll get there, but will be
later than expected. Can't wait
to see you.
Love, Dad
```

Molly didn't say anything. She just handed the telegram to Ricky and sank back against the pillows. *Now Dad isn't even coming,* she thought.

Nothing is working out. Absolutely nothing.

"So," said Ricky with a sigh, "you don't have to get all upset about Dad missing you in the show because you're sick. He won't see *any* of us in the show because he won't be there. It stinks, doesn't it?" He kicked the door with his sneaker. "But Mom keeps saying, 'The show must go on!' So we're all going over to the auditorium later. Mrs. Gilford is coming here to take care of you. I'm supposed to ask if you want anything now."

Molly shook her head no.

"Okay," said Ricky. "Oh, I almost forgot. I'm also supposed to get your Miss Victory costume to bring with us."

"It's all in that suitcase by the closet in my room," said Molly. She thought about how proud she'd felt when Miss LaVonda gave her the suitcase with the costume in it. "Who gets to be Miss Victory?"

"Alison," said Ricky. "I guess because she looks so good in the costume. But everyone knows she's not half as good a dancer as you are," he blurted out. As he hurried out the door, he bumped into Jill.

"I brought your paper dolls and your kaleidoscope," said Jill. "I thought you might be bored up here."

"Thanks," said Molly. Her voice was so hoarse it was a whisper.

"I wish I were the one who was sick," said Jill. "I really do. I'm just in the choir. No one would miss me in the show. But you! You worked so hard to learn that Miss Victory dance and to get your hair just right. It isn't fair. You must be so disappointed."

"Yeah," croaked Molly. "But I'm even more disappointed about Dad not coming home."

"I know," said Jill. "It's very hard to be mature about disappointments like this." She sighed. "I guess I'd better get ready to go. See you later."

After the door was closed, Molly began to yank the bobby pins out of her hair one by one. There was no reason, no reason at all, for curls *now*. Her damp, defeated hair felt like wet snakes, so she braided it up any old which way, just to get it off her shoulders. *Same dumb braids,* she thought. *I'm the same dumb me.* But who cared? There was no reason to be the New Molly anymore. Besides, if she had not been so stupid about curls, she wouldn't have caught cold in the first place. It was her own stupidity that had ruined everything.

In a little while, Mom came in with a glass of ginger ale and some medicine. She looked very beautiful and smelled like perfume. "We've got to hurry off to the show now," she said. "I'm sorry to leave you alone, but Mrs. Gilford missed the bus. She'll be here in about half an hour. And we'll all be home after the show, at about six o'clock. Try to sleep." She kissed Molly on the cheek and squeezed her hand. "I'm really very sorry about all this, dear," she said. And then she left.

The house was very quiet after everyone had gone. Molly played with her paper dolls for a while and looked through the kaleidoscope, but she couldn't get interested in either one. A cheerless

 dusk filled the room. Molly switched on the light. *Probably the only light on in the house,* she thought gloomily. She felt very lonely and very, very sorry for herself. No show. No Miss Victory. And worst of all, no Dad. She had thought everything was going to be so perfect. Perfect, huh!

Molly had thought everything was going to be so perfect.
Perfect, huh! Perfectly awful was more like it.

Perfectly awful was more like it.

And on top of all that, her ears ached and buzzed and didn't even work right. Right now, for instance, she thought she heard the front door opening. But it couldn't be, because it was too soon for Mrs. Gilford and way too soon for everyone to come home from the show. Now she thought she heard someone climbing up the stairs. Dumb ears!

"I'm home!" a voice called out.

It was Dad.

"Dad!" gasped Molly. She pulled back the covers and sprang out of bed. "Dad! Dad! You're home!" She tore out of the room and ran halfway down the stairs, right into Dad's arms. She hugged him so hard his hat fell off and tumbled down the steps. Her nose was squashed against his coat, but she didn't care.

Without a word, Dad hugged Molly for a long, long time. Then he put his hands on her shoulders and just stared at her. Finally he said, "Gosh and golly, olly Molly! You look exactly as I remembered you, just as I've pictured you for two long years. You look perfect!"

Molly grinned. "Perfect!" she said. Then she hugged Dad again.

Absolutely perfect.

LOOKING
BACK
1944

A Peek Into
the Past

Americans welcomed soldiers home in real life, in magazines, and in movies.

In 1945, World War Two ended and times changed for all Americans, even young girls like Molly. Thousands of families were reunited when fathers, brothers, and sons returned from the fighting. Cheering crowds met the ships that brought troops back home. They welcomed the soldiers as heroes. People believed that the whole world would be a better place because American soldiers had fought and won the war.

When the war was over, most Americans' lives returned to normal. Things that had been scarce during the war were plentiful again. Factories that had made guns, bullets, and tanks for the war went back to making refrigerators, washing

Returning soldiers crossed the oceans in troop ships.

*After the war, Americans bought
things that had been scarce.*

machines, and bicycles. People bought these things
quickly because their old ones had worn out during the
war. Factories also made things that most Americans
had never owned before, like cars and television sets.
Before the war, only half of the families in America
owned a car. After the war, nearly every American
family had one. Before the war, most Americans had
never seen a television at all. After the war, television
sets were popular things to buy, even though their
pictures were only in black and white.

During the war, men left
their jobs to become soldiers
and women went to work in
factories doing any job that
needed to be done. But after
the war, most women stopped
working. They saw posters
that told them it was patriotic

GIVE BACK   THEIR JOBS

After the war, so many couples started families that the period was called "the baby boom."

to give their jobs back to the men. Magazines said that women's most important work was caring for children, cooking, and keeping a clean house. Young women were encouraged to marry young, even right after high school. They often had large families of four or five children.

After the war there were not enough places for all of America's new families to live, so whole new towns had to be built. The new towns, called *suburbs*, were built outside of cities. Families who moved to the suburbs needed schools, grocery stores, gas stations, churches, parks, and playgrounds. In the years after the war, all these things were built in the suburbs. Building them made jobs for many returning soldiers.

In some suburbs, all the houses looked the same. They were called *prefab* houses because they were *prefabricated*, or partly built in factories. They were all the

These prefab houses were shipped from the factory in large pieces.

Commuter trains took men from the suburbs to their city jobs.

same because they could be built more quickly that way. People still live in these houses today. To us they may seem small, but after the war families were glad to have any home of their own, even in a suburb far away from their old neighborhoods and their relatives.

After the war, most Americans thought of cities as places to work, not as places for families to live. Men who lived in the suburbs *commuted*, or traveled to their city jobs in cars or trains. Women and children only visited cities occasionally, when they wanted to shop in big department stores or go to museums. Trips to the city were dress-up events. Boys wore jackets and ties. Women and girls wore hats, gloves, and fancy dresses, never playclothes. They felt pretty in long, full skirts after wearing short, skimpier clothing during the war. Women liked being able to wear nylon stockings, which were much more comfortable than the leg make-up some women had worn during the war. But one style that was

Women and girls dressed up when they went to the city to shop.

65

After the war, women wore pants when they relaxed.

popular during World War Two did not change. Women have continued to wear pants ever since then.

Though the war was over, it had been a terrible experience that frightened many people. More people died in World War Two than in any war in history. In places near the fighting, not just soldiers but women, children, and old people were killed by bombs, disease, and starvation. Millions of people were murdered in Nazi concentration camps. After the war, *refugees*—people whose homes had been destroyed—still didn't have food, clothing, or places to live. Whole cities needed to be rebuilt.

When the war ended, Americans wanted all people's lives to return to normal, so the United States took the lead in helping its allies, as well as its enemies, build their countries back up again.

Millions of people died during World War Two. Whole cities were destroyed in Europe and Asia.

America dropped two atomic bombs on Japan before the war was over.

In one important way, however, World War Two changed the lives of all people forever. It was during that war that America dropped the world's first atomic bomb, a bomb so powerful that the world would never be truly safe again. Some families built shelters in their backyards, hoping to be protected if another atomic bomb were ever dropped. Other people, however, knew the real lesson of World War Two was that all people in every country on earth must learn to live together in peace. In 1945, right after the war ended, the United Nations was born. Today, member countries of the United Nations still come together to work out their differences, so that the world will never have to go to war again.

As President Truman watched, America joined the United Nations on June 26, 1945.

THE BOOKS ABOUT MOLLY

MEET MOLLY • An American Girl
While her father is fighting in World War Two,
Molly and her brother start their own war at home.

MOLLY LEARNS A LESSON • A School Story
Molly and her friends plan a secret project to help the
war effort, and learn about allies and cooperation.

MOLLY'S SURPRISE • A Christmas Story
Molly makes plans for Christmas surprises,
but she ends up being surprised herself.

HAPPY BIRTHDAY, MOLLY! • A Springtime Story
An English girl comes to stay with Molly,
but she's not what Molly expects!

MOLLY SAVES THE DAY • A Summer Story
At summer camp, Molly has to pretend to be her
friend's enemy and face her own fears, too.

CHANGES FOR MOLLY • A Winter Story
Dad will return from the war any day! Will he arrive in time
to see the "grown-up" Molly perform as Miss Victory?

◆

WELCOME TO MOLLY'S WORLD • 1944
American history is lavishly illustrated
with photographs, illustrations, and
excerpts from real girls' letters and diaries.

MORE TO DISCOVER!

While books are the heart of The American Girls Collection®, they are only the beginning. The stories in the Collection come to life when you act them out with the beautiful American Girls dolls and their exquisite clothes and accessories. To request a catalogue full of things girls love, you can send in this postcard, call **1-800-845-0005,** or visit our Web site at **americangirl.com**.

Please send me an American Girl catalogue.

My name is _____

My address is _____

City_____ State _____ Zip _____

My birth date is ____ / ____ / ____   E-mail address _____
               Month *Day* *Year*

Parent's signature _____

1961i

And send a catalogue to my friend:

My friend's name is _____

Address _____

City_____ State _____ Zip _____

1225i

If the postcard has already been removed from this book
and you would like to receive an American Girl catalogue,
please send your name and address to:

American Girl
P.O. Box 620497
Middleton, WI 53562-9940

You may also call our toll-free number, **1-800-845-0005,**
or visit our Web site at **americangirl.com**.

BUSINESS REPLY MAIL
FIRST-CLASS MAIL   PERMIT NO. 1137   MIDDLETON WI

POSTAGE WILL BE PAID BY ADDRESSEE

PO BOX 620497
MIDDLETON WI 53562-9940

Tripp, Valerie,
1951-

Changes for Molly.

DATE			